To my parents, Amna and Bilal and my siblings, Anas and Halima.
Once upon a time, we were immigrants. – S. R.

To my little seeds of promise – my kids! – R. M.

Little Seeds
of Promise

Here, Maya thought,
the world was unfriendly and cold.

She felt *so* different.
Maybe it was the way she spoke,
or the lunch she ate,
or the clothes she wore.

Lonely and lost,
she missed the home she had left behind.

There, Maya slept to the
night watchman's song
and woke to the sweet *adhan*.
There, people said
"As-salāmu 'alaykum!"
and danced in the warm monsoon.

There lived Nani,
sweet and tender,
with a hundred wrinkles on her face.

She always smelled like flowers.

Before Maya said goodbye,
Nani gave her a gift–little seeds of promise.
She whispered,
"Bloom where you are planted, Maya."

But Maya didn't know how to do that.

Here, life was not the same.
The ground was so hard, so stubborn.
Her seeds would never blossom.

Not *here.*

Maya carried the seeds with her everywhere she went...

to the post office,

to the library,

and even to school.

But she never showed them to anyone.
Maya guarded them like a secret.

Whenever Maya felt sad,
she closed her eyes and
imagined Nani right *here*.

"Little Maya, dig deep
and plant them," said Nani.
"One day, you'll be
surrounded by flowers."

If only, Maya thought.

There, Nani and Maya
danced,
laughed,

and prayed among flowers.

If her seeds did grow into flowers *here*,
she'd count them like stars in the sky.

Maybe...
Maybe, she could plant a seed.
Only one.

Maya found a patch of earth.

She dug deep, placed her seed, and covered it with dirt.

Maya longed for rain.

But she knew better than to wait for it.

Maya hoped for warmth.

She made way for the rays from the sun.

Days passed and nothing happened.
Maya wished she could crack open
the seed and force it to grow.

But Nani reminded her that
seeds have a long journey
from the ground up.

They need lots of rainfall,
days of sunshine,
and care.

So, Maya greeted her seed with love and kindness.
She sang the night song to it.
She imagined it growing strong.

Before long, Maya felt something whirling inside of her, ready to burst out into the world.

She imagined her seeds growing into little buds,
pretty florets,
and finally, sweet-smelling flowers.

She heard Nani saying,
Little Maya, let your seeds be free!

She loved keeping her seeds of promise safe,
but they needed to stretch out,
    get bigger
            and taller.

Could she be brave enough to let them go?

Could she share them with the world?

Maya smiled.

She was ready to let her seeds grow.

One day, she looked back
and her seeds of promise
stood so tall, so bright,
like hope,
shooting out of the earth toward the sky.

Their blooms smelled
ever so familiar.

Like Nani, over *there*.
Like the warm breeze, *here*.

Like home.

Library of Congress Control Number: 2021938943
ISBN 9781943147939

Text copyright © 2021 by Sana Rafi
Illustrations by Renia Metallinou
Illustrations copyright © 2021 The Innovation Press

Published by The Innovation Press
7511 Greenwood Avenue N. #4132, Seattle, WA 98103
www.theinnovationpress.com

Printed and bound by Worzalla
Production date July 2021

Cover lettering by Nicole LaRue
Cover art by Renia Metallinou
Book layout by Tim Martyn